TIMBERWOLF Hunt

Sigmund Brouwer

illustrated by Dean Griffiths

ORCA BOOK PUBLISHERS

Library and Archives Canada Cataloguing in Publication

Brouwer, Sigmund, 1959-
Timberwolf hunt / written by Sigmund Brouwer ; illustrated by Dean Griffiths.

(Orca echoes)
ISBN 978-1-55143-726-2

I. Griffiths, Dean, 1967- II. Title. III. Series.
PS8553.R68467T45 2007   JC813'.54   C2006-907058-x

First published in the United States, 2007
Library of Congress Control Number: 2006939249

Summary: In this third book in the Timberwolves series, Johnny and Stu must figure out what
to do when the weakest player on their team is getting the most ice time.

MIX
Paper from
responsible sources
FSC™ C016245
www.fsc.org

*Orca Book Publishers is dedicated to preserving the environment and has printed
this book on paper certified by the Forest Stewardship Council.*

Orca Book Publishers gratefully acknowledges the support for its publishing programs
provided by the following agencies: the Government of Canada through the Canada Book Fund
and the Canada Council for the Arts, and the Province of British Columbia through
the BC Arts Council and the Book Publishing Tax Credit.

Typesetting by Christine Toller
Cover artwork and interior illustrations by Dean Griffiths
Author photograph by Bill Bilsley

ORCA BOOK PUBLISHERS
PO Box 5626, Stn. B
Victoria, BC Canada
V8R 6S4

ORCA BOOK PUBLISHERS
PO Box 468
Custer, WA USA
98240-0468

www.orcabook.com
Printed and bound in Canada.

14 13 12 11 • 5 4 3 2

To Dan Kersey: He shoots, he scores!
D.G.

Chapter One
A Trapped Bat

"Shut the door!" Stu Duncan said to Johnny Maverick. "We need help!"

Johnny had just walked into the dressing room with his hockey equipment. Stu was his best friend. They played for the Howling Timberwolves. The team was getting ready to play the Grizzlies.

"I agree that you need help," Johnny said to Stu. "A doctor should see if you still have a brain."

The rest of the players laughed. It looked like Johnny was right.

Stu was standing in the middle of the room. His hockey bag was at his feet. He was holding a hockey stick straight up. He was pushing the butt end of the

stick against the bottom of a plastic bucket. It pressed the top of the bucket against the ceiling.

"I'm standing here for a good reason," Stu said. "I have trapped a bat under the bucket."

"A bat?" Johnny said. "A hairy bat? With wings? And fangs?"

"Bats don't have fangs," Stu said.

"Yes, they do," Johnny said. "Big fangs. Dripping with blood. You should see them in my comic books."

"Johnny," Stu said, "I hate to break it to you. It's like Santa Claus."

"Santa Claus has fangs in your comic books?" Johnny said. "Cool. Can I borrow your comic books?"

"No," Stu said, "Santa Claus is not real. Just like the bats in your comic books. Real bats don't have fangs. Now can you help me?"

Johnny put down his hockey bag. "Sure."

"Good," Stu said. "Hold this stick and press it hard against the bucket. Keep the bat trapped while I get Mr. Gregg."

3

Mr. Gregg was in charge of the arena. He ran the ice-cleaning machine and cleaned the dressing rooms.

"I can get Mr. Gregg if you like," Johnny said.

"Please hold the stick," Stu said. "Let me get Mr. Gregg. My arms are tired. I don't want the bat to get loose."

"All right," Johnny said. "Just make sure that Mr. Gregg doesn't bring Stinky with him. That would be worse than a bat with fangs."

Stinky was Mr. Gregg's dog. It was big and fat and slow. Everyone in the town of Howling knew about Stinky. They knew there was a good reason that Stinky was called Stinky.

"I want to live," Stu said. "I'll make sure Stinky does not come into the dressing room with Mr. Gregg. Now will you hold this bucket for me?"

Johnny took the stick.

Stu stepped away.

"Hey," Johnny said. He looked up at the bucket. "This is heavy!"

Stu did not answer. He pulled his own hockey bag away from Johnny. He moved Johnny's hockey bag closer to Johnny's feet.

"This bucket is heavy!" Johnny said again. "It must be a really big bat!"

"The bucket is filled with water," Stu said. He laughed. "Don't let go or you will get wet! And you will get your hockey bag wet too!"

Everyone else laughed too.

"Water?" Johnny said. He pushed the hockey stick hard against the bottom of the bucket. He did not want to get wet. He did not want to get his hockey bag wet. "You played a trick on me."

"It's a good trick. But it wasn't my idea. It was Tom's."

Tom Morgan was another friend. Johnny had once made him wear a dress to a hockey game, but that was another story.

"Tom's idea?" Johnny said.

Tom was in the corner of the room. He grinned.

"Yes, Johnny," Tom said, "we've played this trick on everyone. They all had turns holding the stick. Stu was the guy who came in just before you did."

"Great," Johnny said. The bucket was heavy. He didn't want all the water to drop on him. He kept pushing hard against the bottom of the bucket. "I'm the last guy."

"No," Tom said, "you are the second last guy. Remember? While Coach Smith is gone, we have a new coach who just moved to Howling. I heard his son plays hockey too."

"Right," Johnny said. "His son is Eldridge Elwell."

Just then, a new kid walked into the dressing room with his hockey bag.

"Hi," the new kid said. He was not too tall and not too short. Not too fat and not too skinny. He had dark hair. He also had a shy smile. "My name is Eldridge. My dad is the new coach. He is going to be here in a few minutes. He just had to park his truck."

"Hi," Johnny said to the new kid. "Glad you're here. I need your help."

"Sure," Eldridge said. "What is it?"

"Well," Johnny said, "I've got a bat trapped under this bucket. Can you keep it trapped while I go get Mr. Gregg? He is in charge of the arena."

"Yes," Eldridge said, "I'll help."

"Good," Johnny said. "Hold this stick and press it hard against the bucket."

Chapter Two
Don't Make the Coach Mad!

"Eldridge," Coach Elwell said. He had just walked into the room. "What are you doing?"

Coach Elwell was a big man. His head was half bald. He had a moustache. He was wearing a suit and a tie. It was the first time the players had seen him. He was Coach Smith's new boss. Coach Elwell was going to be their coach for four weeks while Coach Smith was on vacation. Coach Smith never wore a suit and a tie. Coach Smith would be back for playoffs.

"I'm holding this bucket up against the ceiling," Eldridge said. "If I let go, it—"

"I can see you're pushing a stick up against a bucket," Coach Elwell said. He had a big voice to match his big size. "Didn't I tell you that the first thing you needed to do was fill the water bottles?"

"Yes, but—"

"Don't make excuses," Coach Elwell said. "I expect you to listen to me. Now put that hockey stick down right away."

"Yes, but—"

"Young man, I just said I expect you to listen to me."

"Excuse me," Johnny said to Coach Elwell. "I can explain."

"Did I ask you to interrupt?" Coach Elwell said to Johnny. "All of you should learn right now that I don't like to be interrupted."

"Yes," Johnny said, "but you should let us help Eldridge with the bucket or—"

"Enough," Coach Elwell said to Johnny. "Or you will be benched for the whole game. Players don't tell coaches what to do."

Johnny didn't say another word. He did not want to be benched.

All of the other players were quiet too. Coach Elwell was big. Coach Elwell had a big voice.

Coach Elwell looked at Eldridge. Eldridge was still pushing the bucket against the ceiling. "Put that down this minute!"

"But if I let go of the stick—"

"When will you learn that I don't like back talk?" Coach Elwell said. "Players don't tell coaches what to do. Sons don't tell fathers what to do."

He stepped right up to Eldridge.

"I want you to fill the water bottles," Coach Elwell said to Eldridge. He put his hand on the hockey stick. "Do it now!"

Eldridge held on tight to the hockey stick. "But—"

"Enough!" Coach Elwell said. He yanked the stick from Eldridge's hands. The bucket at the top of the stick fell from the ceiling. It landed on Coach Elwell's head.

It made a clunking sound on his skull. It fit over his head like a helmet. The water soaked his suit and tie.

The room was very quiet.

Except for Johnny Maverick. He remembered what Scooby-Doo would say when something like this happened.

"Ruh-Roh!" Johnny Maverick said in his best Scooby-Doo voice.

Stu and Tom giggled. Coach Elwell had a bucket over his head. He was still holding the hockey stick. His suit was very wet. The rest of the players started to giggle too.

Coach Elwell pulled the bucket off his head. His moustache looked like a drowned mouse.

The room became very quiet again.

"Who played this trick on Eldridge?" he asked. His voice sounded like thunder. He was big and he looked angry.

"He did!" Johnny said, pointing at Tom.

"He did!" Tom said, pointing at Johnny.

"That's it!" Coach Elwell said. "You are both benched for the whole game. You will watch it from the stands."

Chapter Three
The Stinkiest Dog in the World

"Tom," Johnny said. He and Tom were sitting in the stands. "You are disgusting."

The referee was ready to drop the puck. The hockey game between the out-of-town Grizzlies and the hometown Howling Timberwolves was about to begin. Eldridge Elwell was starting at center ice for the Timberwolves. Usually Tom started the game.

"The bucket with water seemed like a good idea at the time," Tom said. "I already told you I'm sorry. How could I know that Coach Elwell would grab the stick?"

"Not that," Johnny said. He sniffed the air. He gagged. "I mean really. Did you have ten pounds of beans for breakfast? You should go into a bathroom if it's that bad."

Tom sniffed the air too. "Yuck, that is disgusting. I promise, it wasn't me."

Tom and Johnny looked at each other.

Then they looked down at the floor beneath the stands.

"It's Stinky," Johnny said, groaning. "Wow. They don't call him that for nothing."

The stands in the arena were the kind that could be pushed back. There was a lot of space beneath them. Often there would be popcorn and litter on the cement floor. Sometimes little kids walked around under the stands looking for lost coins.

Sure enough, there was Stinky. Mr. Gregg's dog was big and fat and slow. And stinky.

Stinky looked up. He saw the boys looking down. He wagged his tail. Maybe they would drop a piece of hot dog by mistake. No one ever dropped food on purpose if Stinky was around.

"Don't feed him," Johnny said. "Then he will follow us no matter where we sit."

Stinky made a long rude noise. The long rude noise didn't come from his front end. Right away the bad smell reached Johnny and Tom.

"Yuck," Tom said. "There he goes again."

It was bad enough that they had been benched from the game. *Now this?*

Tom and Johnny jumped up. They moved to another part of the stands. Just as they sat down, Eldridge Elwell skated into the Grizzlies' zone.

He fell.

He got up. He chased the Grizzlies' center.

He fell. He got up.

"The new player doesn't look that good," Johnny said. He wasn't being mean. He was just stating it like a fact.

"Yes," Tom said, "he needs some different equipment."

"What equipment?" Johnny asked.

"He needs a pillow on his butt," Tom said.

Eldridge got up just in time to receive a pass from one

of the Timberwolves' wingers. The puck landed on his stick. He fell again. It looked like the puck had knocked him over. The Grizzlies' defenseman took the puck and skated to center. The Grizzlies' center stayed close with Eldridge.

The Grizzlies' defenseman passed the puck to a winger. Suddenly, it was a four on two.

The wingers for the Timberwolves tried to catch up. They couldn't. Eldridge tried to catch up. He fell again.

In the Timberwolves' end, the Grizzlies' center dropped back. If Eldridge had been able to keep up, he would have been guarding the Grizzlies' center. Instead the center was wide open for a pass.

The Grizzlies' winger dropped the puck back to the Grizzlies' center.

He was all alone. He took a big slap shot. It bounced off the Timberwolves' goalie. But a Grizzlies winger was there for the rebound. He knocked it into the net.

Just like that, the Timberwolves were down 1–0. Less

than thirty seconds had passed after the start of the game.

"Great," Johnny said to Tom. "You're one of the best players in the league. Without you, the team is in trouble."

"You're one of the best players in the league too," Tom said. "How much worse can it get that we are both benched?"

They heard a loud rude noise.

Johnny sniffed the air. He wanted to throw up.

Tom sniffed the air. He wanted to throw up too.

"That's your answer," Tom said, pointing down at the floor under the stands. Even though they had not given Stinky any food, he had followed them. Stinky wagged his tail, hoping for some food. "It can get a lot worse."

Chapter Four
Honk! Honk!

"Here he comes," Tom whispered to Johnny. "Remember, if we talk to Eldridge when he sits down, he won't notice our trick."

"You shouldn't do it," Stu said. "It's not his fault."

Tom and Johnny and Stu were in their classroom. They were waiting for the bell to ring and for the teacher to arrive. Eldridge Elwell had just walked through the door.

Eldridge saw Tom and Johnny and Stu standing by his desk.

"Hey, guys," he said. He put his books on his desk.

"Sit down," Tom said. "We want to talk to you."

Eldridge sat down. The plan had worked. Eldridge was so busy looking at them that he had not looked down at his chair.

"Sure guys," Eldridge said. "What is it?"

"The Howling Timberwolves have lost four games in a row," Tom said. "You need to do something about it. Now we have to win two out of our last three games. Otherwise we won't make the playoffs."

"I try my hardest," Eldridge said. "I'm just not a good player like you guys."

Stu nodded. Stu wasn't the best player either. He knew what Eldridge felt like.

"We know you try hard," Johnny said. "We like you on our team. But you have to do something about your dad before our game tonight."

"My dad?"

"Yes," Tom said, "your dad is the coach. He puts you on the ice more than any other player."

This was true. When the Timberwolves had a power play, Coach Elwell put Eldridge on the ice. When the Timberwolves were shorthanded, Coach Elwell put Eldridge on the ice. The other coach had always put Johnny and Tom on the ice together to kill penalties or for power plays. But Coach Elwell always made one of them sit on the bench while Eldridge played.

"I am sorry about that," Eldridge said.

"Sorry isn't good enough," Tom said. Tom hated losing games. "You should tell him you don't want to play as much. You don't want the team to keep losing, do you?"

"I don't," Eldridge said.

"Do you like being part of the team?" Johnny asked. He felt sorry for Eldridge too.

"Yes," Eldridge said.

"Do you agree the team would play better if you didn't get so much ice time?" Johnny asked.

"Yes," Eldridge said. "Do you think I like making mistakes when better players should be on the ice?"

"So we agree," Johnny said. "You'll talk to your dad."

"I will think about it," Eldridge said.

"See?" Stu said. "I told you Eldridge was a good guy. We don't need to—"

"Thinking about it isn't good enough," Tom said to Eldridge. Tom hated losing games. "Otherwise things will get worse for you."

"Worse?" Eldridge asked.

"Worse," Tom said. "We like you on our team. You have to help the team win two out of our last three games. We want to make the playoffs."

Before Tom could say anything else, the bell rang. The teacher, Mr. Griswald, walked into the classroom. He took attendance.

"Eldridge," Mr. Griswald said, "could you take the attendance to the office?"

Eldridge stood up.

The girls and boys behind him began to giggle.

Tom had put a piece of paper down on the seat. He had put glue on the top of the paper so that when Eldridge sat down, the paper would stick to his pants.

The trick had worked. The paper was stuck to Eldridge's rear end. The boys and girls behind him saw what Tom had written on the paper.

Honk! Honk!

Eldridge walked to the front of the class. He didn't know why everyone was laughing. Mr. Griswald handed him the sheet without looking up. Now everybody in the classroom except Mr. Griswald saw the paper stuck to his rear end.

Honk! Honk!

Eldridge walked out of the classroom and down the hall with the paper stuck to his rear end. Some other kids were already in the hallway, going to different classrooms.

They began to laugh too.

Honk! Honk!

Chapter Five
Torture Chamber

That night after school, Tom and Johnny and Stu waited for Eldridge outside the dressing room. They stood beside Mr. Gregg's janitor's closet in the hallway at the arena. They knew Eldridge would be at the rink early to fill water bottles for Coach Elwell.

Eldridge walked down the hallway with his equipment. Tom and Stu and Johnny had blocked the hallway with their hockey bags.

"Honk, honk," Tom said.

"Come on," Stu said to Tom. "Remember, he is part of our team."

"That's all right, Stu," Eldridge said. "I thought it was funny. It would have been funnier if the paper had been stuck to someone else's rear end."

"He *is* part of our team," Tom said to Stu. "We like him. All I'm saying is that he should play the same amount as us. Not more."

"You guys are right," Eldridge said.

"Tonight is a big game," Johnny said. "If we don't win, it is going to be very hard to make the playoffs."

"That's right," Tom said. "Have you talked to your dad about not playing so much?"

"Not yet," Eldridge said. "I promise I'll try really hard tonight."

"Trying isn't good enough," Tom said. Tom opened the door to the janitor's closet. He picked up Eldridge's hockey bag. He shoved the bag into the closet. He slammed the door.

29

"What's going on?" Eldridge said.

"Just putting your bag in a safe place," Tom said.

"Honk, honk on the rear end is funnier," Eldridge said. He opened the door to get his bag. Tom pushed him inside and shut the door.

"Hey!" Eldridge said. "It's dark in here. I can't see a thing."

The light switch was in the hallway. Tom did not turn on the light for Eldridge.

Eldridge tried to open the door. But Tom had pushed a wedge of wood under the door. It would not open.

"Guys?" Eldridge said. "Are you still there?"

"Yes," Tom said. "Are you going to talk to your dad? Or do we have to leave you in the torture chamber?"

"This is a closet," Eldridge said. "It's not a—"

There was a long rude noise inside the closet.

"What was that?" Eldridge asked. Then Eldridge was quiet for a couple of seconds. "Yuck. What's that smell?"

"Let him out," Stu whispered to Tom. "Nobody should have to face that kind of torture."

Johnny wanted to agree with Stu. The smell was coming out from under the door. It was a horrible smell.

Tom shook his head. "Eldridge has to talk to his dad. None of the rest of us can."

"Yuck!" Eldridge said again. "It's like an outhouse. Except ten times worse. It's…"

Eldridge screamed. "It's alive!"

Eldridge screamed again. "It's licking me!"

Johnny knocked on the door. "Eldridge, it's just Mr. Gregg's dog. Stinky. He's a very nice dog. He wouldn't hurt anything."

"He takes up a lot of room," Eldridge said. "And he keeps licking my hand. Let me out."

"I wouldn't worry about how much room he takes up," Johnny said. "Or how much he licks your hand. I would worry about something else instead."

There was that sound again inside the closet. That long rude sound. It did not come from the front end of Stinky.

"That's what I would worry about," Johnny said.

"Oh, disgusting!" Eldridge said. "Is there a cork in here?"

"Come on," Tom said to Eldridge. "We like you. We know you try hard. We want you on the team. We just want you to tell your dad not to give you so much ice time."

There was another long rude noise.

"Doesn't this dog eat anything else except for beans?" Eldridge yelled.

Tom and Johnny and Stu did not answer. At the end of the hallway, they saw Coach Elwell turn the corner. He was talking to one of the parents.

"We'd better go," Tom said. "Before Coach Elwell sees us here."

Tom leaned over and pulled the wedge out from the

door. He looked back down the hallway. Coach Elwell had stopped. He was still talking to the parent.

Tom and Johnny and Stu picked up their hockey bags. They walked toward the dressing room. As they walked away, they heard the long rude noise from inside the closet again.

"Guys?" Eldridge called out. "Guys? Help. I think I'm dying in here. This dog should be a weapon in the army."

They kept walking.

Chapter Six
A Very Lost Skate

"Why in the world would you be in a closet with a dog?" Coach Elwell yelled at Eldridge. He had his son by the arm in front of all the players in the dressing room. "Do you have any idea how stupid I looked?"

"You?" Eldridge asked.

"Me? I'm the coach. My own son is in a closet with a dog, yelling for help when I walk by with one of the parents. In the closet in the dark. And all you had to do was open the door."

Coach Elwell kicked the garbage can.

"Sorry," Eldridge said.

"Well?" Coach Elwell said.

"Well what?" Eldridge said.

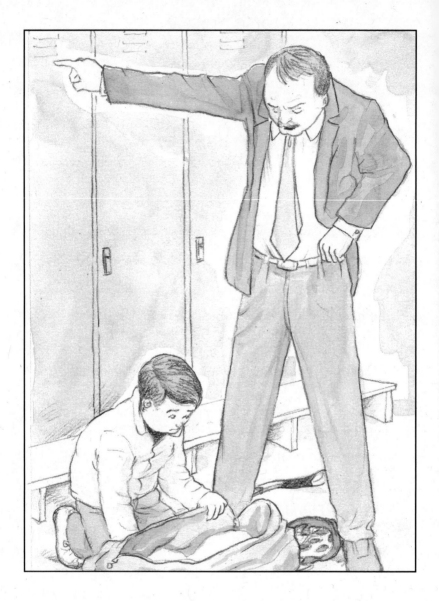

"Why were you in the closet with a dog? You were supposed to be filling water bottles."

"Oh," Eldridge said.

"Well?" Coach Elwell said.

Johnny looked at Tom. Tom looked at Johnny.

Johnny knew what Tom was thinking. Tom knew what Johnny was thinking.

If Eldridge told Coach Elwell what had happened, they would be benched again.

"I'm waiting," Coach Elwell said. "Did you think it was a bathroom?"

"A bathroom?" Eldridge said.

"It smelled horrible in there," Coach Elwell said. "My own son. You made me really look bad."

"The dog's name is Stinky," Eldridge said. "He stinks."

"So once and for all, answer me," Coach Elwell said. "Why would you be in a closet in the dark with a stinky dog yelling for help when all you had to do was open the door?"

Johnny looked at Tom again. Tom looked at Johnny. Eldridge looked at Johnny. Eldridge looked at Tom.

Johnny knew what Tom was thinking. Tom knew what Johnny was thinking. Eldridge knew what Tom and Johnny were thinking.

If Eldridge told Coach Elwell what had happened, they would be benched again.

"I got lost in the closet," Eldridge said. "The dog seemed lonely, and when I went inside, the door shut. I got lost in there because it was so dark."

Coach Elwell kicked the garbage can again. He took a deep breath.

He smiled at Eldridge. "There, I feel much better."

Johnny looked at Tom. Tom looked at Johnny. They felt much better too. It wasn't fun being yelled at by Coach Elwell.

"I'm sorry for making you look bad," Eldridge told Coach Elwell. "You should probably bench me for it."

"Players never tell coaches what to do," Coach Elwell said. "Now get dressed for the big game."

"Sure," Eldridge said. He found a place to sit. He opened his bag. He began to throw his stuff on the floor.

"Oh no," Eldridge said. He threw the rest of his stuff on the floor. "I can't find one of my skates!"

"Are you sure?" Coach Elwell said.

There was all of Eldridge's equipment. But only one skate.

"I'm sure," Eldridge said. "It must have been that dog when I was in the closet. I'll bet he took the skate. You smelled how stinky it was in the closet. That dog probably eats anything. Maybe he thinks the leather will taste good."

Coach Elwell kicked the garbage can.

"Go out there and find the skate," Coach Elwell said, "or you won't be playing hockey tonight."

Chapter Seven
Thank You, Stinky!

Halfway through the third period, it was seven to three
for the Timberwolves against the Leafs. Tom had scored
two goals out of the seven, and Johnny had scored two
goals.

But now the Timberwolves were a man short. Stu had
just taken a penalty for tripping.

Coach Elwell sent Johnny and Tom onto the ice to
kill the penalty.

"Just like old times," Tom said to Johnny as they
skated to the face-off circle on the right side in the
Timberwolves' zone. "You and me."

"Yes," Johnny said, "thanks to Stinky. I never thought
I'd say this. But I like that dog."

"I know," Tom said. "After the game, I'm going to give Stinky three hot dogs for taking Eldridge's skate and hiding it."

"Too bad Eldridge is in so much trouble with his dad," Johnny said. "He's spent all game looking for it. Coach Elwell is sure going to yell at Eldridge on the way home."

"But we're winning," Tom said. "Doesn't it feel good?"

Johnny nodded. "Let's kill this penalty."

"No," Tom said, "let's score a shorthanded goal and put this game away."

Tom reached the face-off circle. He leaned on his stick and got ready for the puck. The Leaf center got ready too.

When the referee dropped the puck, Tom knocked it out of the air toward Johnny. Johnny turned his body into the Leaf winger beside him and kept the winger from getting the puck.

Tom broke toward open ice, halfway to the blue line.

The Leaf center moved toward Johnny to help the Leaf winger fight Johnny for the puck. Johnny saw the center coming. He kicked the puck between the center's skates. The puck reached Tom.

Johnny squirted between the center and the winger and jumped forward.

The Leaf defenseman on Johnny's side was moving toward Tom to stop him. That was a mistake. The defenseman should have backed up instead of pinching in.

Tom saw that the defenseman had trapped himself too far inside the blue line. He flicked a backhand pass back to Johnny, who was moving at full speed along the boards.

The Leaf defenseman turned around, but to catch Johnny, he had to start from standing still. He didn't have a chance.

But Tom had been moving forward anyway, and it was easy for him to keep going forward and pull away from the first Leaf defenseman. Now Johnny and Tom had a two-on-one against the final Leaf defenseman!

They skated at full speed as they crossed the center line.

Johnny stayed wide with the puck and crossed the blue line into the Leaf's zone. The Leaf defenseman had to move to that side of the ice or Johnny would have a breakaway.

Tom slowed down a little. That was better than skating full speed and keeping the defenseman between them. Now it was easy for Johnny to flip a pass back to Tom.

Tom faked a slap shot, and the Leaf defenseman went back toward him to stop it.

Johnny kept streaking and cut in toward the goalie. Tom put the puck on his stick. Johnny snapped the puck into the right side of the net.

Shorthanded goal! Eight to three for the Timberwolves!

And not enough time left in the game for the Leafs to score five goals to catch them!

Johnny raised his stick to celebrate. As he swung around the corner to give Tom a high five, he noticed someone under the stands.

He wasn't sure, but it looked like Eldridge.

With Stinky beside him.

That couldn't be, Johnny thought. Nobody would ever want to spend time hiding under the stands with Stinky.

He didn't have much time to wonder. Tom reached him and slapped his back.

"Great goal," Tom said. "Just like old times!"

Johnny looked back under the stands. He didn't see anybody.

"Yes," Johnny said to Tom, "just like old times."

Chapter Eight
A Not-So-Lost Skate

Johnny Maverick was the last player in the dressing room.

Even though they had won, Coach Elwell was in a bad mood. He had left early with his son. The rest of the players were happy. They sat around and joked for a while, until one by one, they left.

Johnny wasn't as happy as he thought he would be. He had scored three goals, and the Timberwolves had won. Now they only needed to win one more game to make the playoffs. And they had two games left to play in the next two weeks. By then, Coach Smith would be back from vacation.

But Johnny kept remembering what he had seen after

scoring the shorthanded goal. Could that have been Eldridge hiding under the stands with Stinky? But why? Eldridge knew he was in big trouble for losing the skate. He should have been looking for it. He should not have been hiding under the stands with the thief. Especially when the thief was so smelly that it left a green cloud everywhere it went.

Johnny began to throw his equipment into his hockey bag.

The door opened.

"Hi, Mr. Gregg," Johnny said.

Mr. Gregg was an older man with gray hair. He wore a parka all the time, even though it wasn't that cold in the arena.

"Hi, Johnny," Mr. Gregg said. He stood in the doorway. "Sorry. I didn't know you were in here. I was just going to lock up."

Stinky walked into the dressing room. Stinky was always looking for food. Anywhere.

"Just getting ready to go," Johnny said.

There was a long rude noise inside the dressing room. It did not come from the front end of Stinky.

"Yes, sir," Johnny said, jumping up and dragging his hockey bag to the door. "Getting ready to go now."

Too late. The smell nearly knocked Johnny over. He couldn't believe Mr. Gregg didn't notice. But Mr. Gregg had had Stinky for years. The smell never seemed to bother him.

"Johnny?" Mr. Gregg said. "I found something I need to ask you about."

"Sure," Johnny said. "Could we talk in the hallway?"

Mr. Gregg followed Johnny into the hallway. Johnny was glad that Mr. Gregg left Stinky inside the dressing room. Still, some of the smell leaked out from under the door. Johnny pressed an arm against his nose.

"I found a skate," Mr. Gregg said. "I heard that Eldridge was looking for his skate and had to miss the game."

Johnny nodded from behind his arm. "It must be Eldridge's skate. Where did Stinky leave it?"

Mr. Gregg frowned. "Stinky didn't take it."

"He must have taken it," Johnny said. "Eldridge looked all over for it."

"I found it on the top shelf in my janitor's closet," Mr. Gregg said. "It was under an old blanket that I use to wipe oil off the ice-cleaning machine. Do you think Stinky put it there? Or did someone on your team hide it there to keep Eldridge from playing?"

Johnny blinked a couple of times. It wasn't from the smell. It was from surprise.

"Good question, Mr. Gregg," Johnny said. "I'll see what I can find out."

Chapter Nine
I Love Stinky

Johnny met Eldridge at school the next morning before classes started.

"I found your skate," Johnny said.

"I don't believe it," Eldridge said.

"Because you thought you did such a good job of hiding it," Johnny asked, "while you were in the closet yelling for us to let you out?"

Eldridge looked at the floor.

"I won't tell anyone," Johnny said. "Especially Coach Elwell."

"My dad is very angry with me," Eldridge said. "He wasn't going to buy me new skates until I earned enough money to pay for half."

"You knew that would happen, but you still hid the skate," Johnny said.

"You should have thrown my skate away," Eldridge said. "Then I would have missed the next two games, and the Timberwolves would make the playoffs."

"I won't lie to you," Johnny said. "I was tempted."

"I try my hardest," Eldridge said, "but I'm not as good as my dad wants me to be."

"Plus, players should never tell coaches what to do, right?"

"Right," Eldridge said. "That's the way he coaches."

"So you would rather be in trouble with him for losing a skate than for telling him what to do?"

"Yes," Eldridge said. "What else could I do to help the team? Please go and hide my skate, and don't let anyone know you found it."

"I can't do that," Johnny said.

"Why not?" Eldridge asked.

"Because you wanted to help the team so much

that you let your dad yell at you for getting lost in the closet. You didn't tell him that Tom and I locked you in there."

"We need to make the playoffs," Eldridge said. "Remember?"

"I remember that you wanted to help the team so much that you hid under the stands with a dog as stinky as Stinky," Johnny said.

"It was bad," Eldridge admitted. "How can a dog have that much gas? He could fill a hot air balloon."

"That's what I mean," Johnny said. "You really are a team player. You deserve to play and to help us make it to the playoffs."

"But I'm not good enough."

"Maybe not right now," Johnny said. "But our next game isn't for a week. And the next one after that is another week away. That gives us two weeks to help you get better. After that, Coach Smith will be back. Then it won't be a problem for you or us."

"Us?" Eldridge said.

"The whole team," Johnny said. "When I told them how badly you wanted to help us, they thought you should keep playing too."

"Even Tom?" Eldridge said.

"Especially Tom," Johnny said. "And that's a good thing."

"Why?" Eldridge asked.

"You have to ask?" Tom said. He had sneaked up behind Eldridge.

Eldridge jumped.

"I'm the one who can teach you the most," Tom said. "I'm one of the best centers in the league. That's not bragging. It's just a fact."

"Thanks, guys," Eldridge said. "This means a lot to me."

"No problem," Tom said. He patted Eldridge on the back. "See you on the ice."

Eldridge walked away.

"We're going to make the playoffs, aren't we?" Johnny said.

"Of course we are," Tom said. "The whole team is going to help him get better."

"So did you really have to put that piece of paper on his back when you patted him?" Johnny asked.

Eldridge was partway down the hall. Already some kids were starting to laugh. He didn't know it, but he had a sign on his back, a sign with a special message:

I ♥ Stinky.

"Of course I had to do it," Tom said. "He's part of the team."

Sigmund Brouwer loves hockey. He is a bestselling novelist who also writes many books for children and young adults. Sigmund loves visiting schools and talking to students about reading and writing. He and his family divide their time between homes in Red Deer, Alberta, and Nashville, Tennessee.

Sigmund enjoys visiting schools to talk about his books. Interested teachers can find out more by emailing authorbookings@coolreading.com.